STAR DIMMER

PJ GRAY

SADDLEBACK
EDUCATIONAL PUBLISHING

MONARCH JUNGLE®

SADDLEBACK
EDUCATIONAL PUBLISHING
www.sdlback.com

ISBN: 978-1-68021-596-0
eBook: 978-1-63078-973-2

Printed in Malaysia
28 27 26 25 24   2 3 4 5 6

MONARCH
JUNGLE®

She walks in beauty, like the night
Of cloudless climes and starry skies;
And all that's best of dark and bright
Meet in her aspect and her eyes;
Thus mellowed to that tender light
Which heaven to gaudy day denies.

(from "She Walks in Beauty," Lord Byron)

Chapter 1

DRAMA MAMA

Jen Conrad felt like a sleepwalker. Days and hours flowed together. Only her dark roots showed the passing of time. She needed to visit a stylist. But her costly blonde highlights did not matter anymore. Jen was too busy worrying about her life. She was only 17. Yet she felt 70.

Downstairs, her mother was on speakerphone. It was on full blast, of course. Voices carried through the house.

"I know, I know," her mom said. "Look, Jack. I can't deal with this right now. I have a new gig. It's a prime-time network show. I'm working 16-hour days! Jen was better off with you. You're her father. Can't you and Todd take her back? Just for a little while?"

Sleep faded. Her mother's voice made Jen bristle. Jen rolled out of bed. The gray bathrobe called to her. Its color matched her mood. Pulling it on, she walked down the hall. She loved her grandmother's house. The top of the stairs overlooked an open living room. One wall was all windows. They displayed an ocean view.

Jen looked down at her mother. Val was a small woman. She bounced from foot to foot, staring out a window.

"No way, Val," Jack Conrad replied. "We can't. Jen doesn't listen to us. She ran away twice when she was here last. Lately, the press won't leave us alone. We have been stalked. They even upset the poor dogs."

Jen rolled her eyes.

Her mom tried hard to convince Jack. "I know. But she's better now."

Jen smirked. *Better? It's not me who needs to change.*

Her dad was never on her side. He believed all the stories in the press. The tabloids wrote ugly things about Jen. Jack accepted them as fact. None of them were true. But her dad did not care. That led to way too many fights.

"No, Val," he said.

"Please! I can't keep her with me. My place in Los Angeles is too small. Besides, the press is still watching her. She can't keep staying here at the beach. My mother can't deal with her. Babe is too old for this. She doesn't need to worry about photographers popping up everywhere."

"No," he said again. "We can't do it. Jen is all yours." The line went dead.

"Jack? Jack!" A growl erupted from Val. She threw the phone onto a sofa. Jen's mom was all about drama.

Chapter 2

"IT" GIRL

Jen looked around. She felt empty. This was Babe's beach house. Babe was her grandmother. The place was giant. As a child, Jen had spent time there. Then came boarding school. Modeling was next. Traveling became her life.

Babe's house was in Malibu. Jen had grown up in Beverly Hills. It was about 25 miles away. But it felt *so* far. Los Angeles did too. That was where Val now lived.

Jen walked back down the hallway. An open door stopped her. It was her mom's old bedroom. Jen slowly stepped inside.

Pictures of Val were everywhere. They covered the walls. The dresser and desk were filled too. In the photos, her mom laughed with friends. Movie stars hugged her. It was a Val Kane shrine.

Jen picked up a frame. She wiped dust from the glass. It was a photo of her mom. She was with David Bowie. They were backstage at a concert. Val was a teenager. Her smile was huge. She looked like an adoring fan. Bowie appeared cool and distant.

Trophies and school ribbons were on the shelves. Jen moved through the room. Her fingers brushed the awards. A gold trophy stood in the center of the shelf. The label read "Val Kane, Miss LA County Teen." The tall trophy next to it read "Val Kane, Miss Beverly Hills 1990." That summed up her mom at age 17.

Jen shook her head. She was nothing like her mother. *Thank goodness*, she thought.

Val Kane had grown up a Hollywood kid. Her dad, Ben Kane, was a filmmaker. He wasn't a big one. But he was famous enough. Val had been primed for a movie career. She was beautiful. Her dark hair was silky. Stunning blue eyes defined her. Magazines dubbed her an "it" girl. Casting directors wanted her. Pageant judges loved her. Val charmed them all.

Life was one big party. Hollywood socialites needed Val. Events filled her calendar. Everyone wanted to be where she went. It was called the "Kane effect."

Val met Jack Conrad at her 20th birthday party. She had just landed her first commercial.

Jack was a stuntman from Utah. He was one of the best in the business. The man was Hollywood handsome too. His good looks were rugged.

Jen knew her mom's first words to her dad. The story had been shared many times. Val had asked, "May I touch your biceps?" Then she grabbed his arm. The thought made Jen cringe.

The couple had a whirlwind romance. Then Val Kane became Mrs. Jack Conrad. Her career soon took off. A walk-on part in a Coppola film was first. Next was a speaking part in a teen hit. Two more films followed. Then came her big break. She landed a role in an Eastwood film. Critics liked her work. Awards followed. Her star was rising.

But Val had a problem. Mood swings ruled her life. Doctors said it was bipolar disorder. Her mood shifted wildly. Pills helped. But Val didn't like taking them. Sometimes she drank alcohol. That made the mood swings worse. Jack tried to care for her. But Val never let him. She also wouldn't help herself. This finally ruined her marriage. It almost wrecked her career. She got better for a short time. A therapist helped.

Val needed to save her marriage. Having a baby seemed like a solution. Then Jen was born. But the damage was done. The star tried juggling motherhood with work. That wasn't easy. Work was hard to get. Even worse, motherhood didn't come naturally to Val.

Jack and Val could not make it work. They divorced. Then Jen was sent to an East Coast boarding school. "Mama has to work," Val had told her.

A few years later, Jack left the film business. Stunt work aged a body quickly. He met a film producer named Todd. They fell in love. First, New York City became their home. Finally, they settled in Connecticut. By then, Jen rarely visited. Jack and Todd owned a big mansion. Three pampered pets were their babies. Jen thought their house was boring. It had spoiled dogs and too many rules. She could only stand visiting during the holidays.

"Jen!" Val shouted from the living room. "Where are you?"

Jen set the trophy down. She walked back to her room. *What now?*

Chapter 3

BIG BREAK

The view of the Pacific Ocean put Jen into a trance. She stared at the waves from her bedroom window. The sun felt warm through the glass. Jen knew what she was about to face. Soon her mother would find her. Then the peace would be broken.

Sunlight filled her room. Memories of the past year flooded in. A stranger had changed her life. Was it just a year ago? It felt like a lifetime.

Jen had returned to Los Angeles for high school. She had few friends at Goldwyn Prep. Kim was her only close friend. Mainly, Jen kept to herself. The school kids didn't impress her. Most girls disliked her. But she never knew why. The guys at school were jerks.

One day, Jen and Kim were in a shoe store on Rodeo Drive. A man in a suit tapped Jen on the shoulder. He quickly studied her face. Then he admired her hair. Jen was surprised when he asked to take her picture.

She was bothered at first. A man approaching a teenager was weird. *What a creep. Who is this person?*

Then the man handed her a business card. He was a scout for a famous modeling agency. After that, things happened fast. Val agreed to let the agency interview Jen. In fact, her mom was thrilled. "I've never been so proud of you!" she gushed.

Then came the photo shoots. Finally, Jen signed with the agency. They wanted her in Japan. The company asked her to quit school. Jen was surprised.

But Val did not hesitate. "Yes!" her mom said. "Don't wait! This is your big break. You can get your GED later."

Before she could argue, Jen was shipped to Tokyo. She was under 18. This meant she needed a chaperone. A woman named Nev was chosen. But Jen never saw her. Nev only called or texted.

In Tokyo, Jen was also assigned a roommate. Cammie had been in Tokyo for two months on her own. The agency was marketing her as the next top model. But Cammie was better. She was 18 and a total beauty. The girl did not have a care in the world. Cammie was always upbeat. Having a good time was her goal.

Cammie loved Tokyo. She was eager to show the

city to the new girl. Jen did her best to keep up. But Cammie was always on the go. They became close friends.

The girl had changed Jen's life forever—in the worst way.

"Jen!" Val called from the doorway. "Did you hear me? We have to talk."

Jen shook off the memory. She kept staring out the window as Val spoke.

Her mother took a long breath. "You need to stay here with Babe for a while. She has more room. My condo is too small. Rob is staying there now. I know you don't like him. Plus, the press is still after you. The last place you need to be is LA. I'm also hiring a tutor. You need to finish school. No arguments about that."

Val's cell phone rang. "It's the studio," she said. "I have to take this." She turned and left the room.

"It's always the studio," Jen said under her breath.

She continued to stare at the ocean. The sun reflected off the window. Jen studied her face in the glass. There were dark circles under her eyes. Her mother was right. She could not go back to LA. The press would never leave her alone.

Sounds of her past came roaring back.

Flashes popped nonstop during photo shoots. They were blinding. *Pop*. Each one sounded like a punch. *Pop*.

"Girl. Hey, you! Girl! What is her name? Hey, girl! What is it? Jen? Jen, honey? Turn your head to the left. I said left. Not that much. That's it."

Pop.

"Relax. You're doing great. That's it."

Pop.

"Love it. Tilt your head. That's it. Hold it!"

Pop.

"Now look at me. Relax more. Hold it. Don't blink."

Pop.

"That's good. Now soften your face."

Pop.

"No! I said soften. Stop wasting my time. Listen to me! Okay, hold it. That's it."

Pop.

"You're doing great. Someone turn that second light down."

Chapter 4

FINDERS
KEEPERS

The sun had set. Jen's bedroom was dark. Her breath caught. Sweat beaded on her forehead. It was getting harder to breathe. *Oh no*, Jen thought. *Not another panic attack. I need air.*

Downstairs, Jen pulled open a sliding glass door. She pushed her way through. The door snapped back. It had caught her bathrobe. Feeling trapped, she gasped. The house would not let her go. Jen yanked at the robe. But it did not budge. In a fit, she ripped it loose. *Finally, I'm free.* She ran across the stone patio. The beach called to her.

Dusk was her favorite time. Shades of orange painted the sky. A few deep breaths steadied her. An ocean breeze calmed her. Waves crashed onto the sand. The thick gray robe was soft against her skin. Her toes dug into the warm sand.

Suddenly she felt something between her toes. It was a necklace. Jen picked it up. She wiped off the sand and looked at it closely. It was a gold chain. A thin, flat piece of metal was attached.

The heart-shaped charm was gold. It was a symbol of love. Jen held it tightly. But she felt nothing. Romance did not interest her. Still, she put the chain around her neck. *Maybe I can pawn it. I need the cash.*

She hated relying on Val for money. Her mom gave her a small allowance. That made Jen mad. She had earned her own money. But she wasn't 18. So Val held control of it. Jen felt like she was in jail at times.

She was not ready to go back to the house. The sound of the waves calmed her. But something pricked Jen's senses. Someone else was there. A man stood a short distance away. He was close to the rocks. His eyes were on the horizon.

Light was waning. Jen struggled to see the man clearly. He was wearing a white hoodie and shorts. Jen tried to catch a glimpse of his face. *Be cool. Do not give this guy the wrong idea.*

The man caught her glance. Jen waved politely. He smiled. Then he waved back.

Quickly, she looked toward the ocean again. Her thoughts raced. *Where did this guy come from? What is he expecting? Did someone from the tabloids track me down?*

The patio lights came on. That was Babe's signal. It meant she needed something. She was looking for Jen.

Jen was not sure what to do. *I don't want to walk back now. Then this guy will know where I live.* Maybe she could just walk away. She would not look in his direction.

Finally, Jen turned. She walked toward the house. Soon, she reached the patio. Jen pushed hair away from her face. Quickly, she glanced in the stranger's direction. He was gone.

Chapter 5

CALL ME BABE

Stars twinkled in the night sky. Jen climbed the stone steps. Waves crashed behind her. The patio lights cut through the darkness. She turned to the beach one last time. *Where did that man go?* Shrugging, she went inside.

Jen felt for the necklace. The metal warmed to her touch. It was her secret treasure. She was not ready for anyone to see it.

"Jen?" Babe called from upstairs. "Is that you?"

"Yes," she called back. "I was just on the beach."

"I want to talk to you." Her grandmother's voice sounded strong. "I'm in my studio."

Jen went upstairs. Then she walked down the hall.

Babe's bedroom was huge. Half of it was used as an art studio. One wall was all windows. There was a large wooden easel. The ocean view was the perfect backdrop. Paintings and canvases were stacked against the walls. Paint tubes and brushes covered the table.

Across the room, Babe rested on her bed. A crossword puzzle held her attention. Her long gray hair was pulled into a neat bun. White silk pajamas draped her thin frame.

Jen stood in the doorway. She looked around. Babe did not glance up.

Emma Kane was Babe's real name. She was a natural beauty. Jen and Val had inherited her big blue eyes. Babe was the only child of a wealthy banker. Her father—Jen's great-grandfather—had backed Ben Kane's first movie. Kane had then dated and married Babe.

The older woman was not a typical mother or grandmother. Babe was kind but guarded. She refused to be labeled a grandmother.

"Just call me Babe," she'd said to Jen long ago. So that was what Jen had done her whole life. She wished that she had spent more time with Babe. At least they were close now. This made Jen happy.

Babe looked up. "There you are!"

Jen smiled. She suddenly felt sloppy. Her windswept hair fell into her eyes.

"Quick," Babe said. "What is a five-letter word for necklace?"

Jen grabbed her bathrobe collar. She pulled it tightly around her neck. "Um. Chain?" Heat rose in her cheeks.

"Chain! Of course." Babe scribbled. Then she tossed the crossword onto the bed. "Enough of that. Come. Sit with me."

Jen sat on the edge of Babe's large bed.

"Now, turn. Face that wall." Her grandmother grabbed a sketchpad from her bedside table. "I want to draw you."

"What?" Jen panicked. "No! I'm a mess."

"Nonsense." Babe began drawing. "Do what you're told." She winked.

Smiling, Jen sat up straighter. Then she turned to the wall.

Babe drew for a few moments. Finally, she spoke. "You know you'll be staying here a while. Correct?"

Jen nodded. "Are you okay with that?"

"Of course," Babe said. "I think it's wise. At least until the press backs off."

"Right." Jen wanted to change the subject. "That big painting in the living room—the one over the fireplace—is that you?"

A soft smile tugged at Babe's lips. "Yes." She continued to sketch. "You like it? It was painted by David Hockney."

Jen did not react. The name didn't ring a bell.

"Hockney," Babe said again. "David Hockney? He

is very famous. Look him up. In fact, the LA County Museum of Art wants that painting."

Jen shrugged. "Okay."

Babe rolled her eyes. "My dear, we need to get you to an art museum. You need culture. Didn't they teach you anything in high school?"

Jen smiled while staring at the wall. "May I ask you a personal question?"

"Go ahead," Babe said.

"Do you have any friends?" She realized how rude that sounded. "Wait. That came out wrong."

Babe laughed. She stayed focused on her sketchpad. "I have a few friends left. When I divorced your grandfather, I lost many of them. He tried to ruin my name. But at least I kept the beach house." Babe stopped drawing and looked up. "What about you? Don't you still have friends from school?"

Jen thought of Kim. Then she shrugged. "I've lost touch with the few I had."

"Maybe it's time to connect with them again. It wouldn't hurt." Her grandma returned to sketching.

"Why did you want to keep this house?" Jen asked.

"Are you kidding?" Babe swung her arm around in a big circle. "Just look. We're at the far end of Malibu. It is very private out here. Plus, the state owns the surrounding land. No one can ever build there. I like the isolation."

That was something they had in common. "May I ask another personal question?"

"Sure."

"Did you love your husband?"

Babe paused. Her drawing stopped. She thought for a moment. "No. I didn't. But I was in love once. Truly in love. Madly and deeply in love."

Jen turned to her grandmother. "When? With who?"

"It was 1966. I was only 22 years old. But I was already unhappy in my marriage. That was when I met someone else." Her eyes took on a faraway look. "He was 20. He loved to surf."

"What happened to him?"

"He went to war. Vietnam. I never saw him again. He died there."

Jen could not speak. Her grandmother's honesty surprised her.

Babe looked across her room to the wall of windows. "He was like the North Star out there. So bright. Then his light went out too quickly. Most stars fade, you know? Like your mother. They flicker a bit. Then they slowly dim and burn out. But his star never had the chance to really shine."

Jen watched Babe's face. It looked peaceful. She wanted to say something. But she felt awkward. What could she say? Nothing would bring back her grandmother's true love. "Would you like to take a walk on the beach?"

Babe shook her head slowly. Then she smiled. "No, thank you. I don't go out there much anymore. I get too out of breath. Besides, the view is great from here."

"Don't you get scared living out here by yourself?"

"No." Babe winked. "I have protection."

Did her grandmother have a gun? Jen didn't know if Babe was joking. "Really? Are you packing heat?" she asked with a chuckle. "Should I be worried?"

"Not unless you plan to rob me."

Chapter 6

SCRAMBLED

Jen woke. Sleep had been restless. She rolled over. The clock read 3:15. It was already late afternoon. Her days and nights must be mixed up. Even a cool shower did not help.

She dressed quickly. It was chilly. Jen chose her favorite cashmere sweater. Sweatpants made her feel cozy.

Downstairs, she made eggs and toast. That was the only thing Cammie had known how to cook. Thoughts of Jen's old roommate twisted her stomach in knots. She recalled the last time she'd seen her old roomie. Cammie had been leaving their apartment for another night out.

"Hey, I'm going to meet up with that guy." Cammie clasped a silver bracelet to her wrist. "You know? The one I danced with last night. He's down to party. Want to come?"

"No. You go."

"Come on, Jen. He's bringing friends." Cammie winked. "They're cute."

Jen yawned. "I'm tired. Plus, we have a photo shoot tomorrow. Early. How do you have so much energy?"

Cammie just rolled her eyes. She plopped on her bed. "Modeling is not so important. Other things are. You should know that."

"What is that supposed to mean?" Jen was not in the mood for a riddle.

Cammie sighed. "Modeling is my mom's dream. Not mine. I want to live for me. Don't you?"

Jen could relate. "I do want to live my own dream. But I don't see what partying has to do with that."

"Not just partying." Cammie jumped up. Then she danced around. "Living. Finding love. Don't you want to meet somebody? Maybe we could both find someone rich! Then we would never have to work again!"

Jen laughed and let Cammie grab her hand. "I think we want different things. My goal is to be happy with me. I want to do that first. I'll worry about love later."

Cammie realized she'd lost the battle. She dropped Jen's hand. "Okay, then. Suit yourself."

For a long moment, Cammie stared at Jen. Finally,

she gave her a fierce hug. "I love you, Jen. Don't wait up."

That was the last thing Jen's roommate had said to her. One thing about the memory bothered her: It seemed like Cammie had been saying goodbye.

Chapter 7

ALL BETS
ARE OFF

Jen shook off the memory. Something bad had happened. There was no way Cammie had run away.

She looked at her cold eggs and toast. Jen thought about what Babe had said. Maybe it wouldn't hurt to try reconnecting with old friends.

Jen went back to her room. She grabbed her phone. High school had been rough. Many girls hated her. Some had spread rumors. She'd never understood why.

A name came to mind: Kim. She was the friend Jen had been closest to. Jen missed her. It had been too long since they'd spoken. She texted Kim. Then her phone buzzed. "This number is out of service."

Quickly, she googled Kim's mom. In a moment, Jen had her number. A woman answered after one ring.

"Hi. Mrs. Allen? This is Jen Conrad. I am looking for Kim. Is she there?"

"Jen? Oh my goodness! How are you?" Mrs. Allen sounded happy. That made Jen smile.

She found out that Kim was visiting her aunt. But Mrs. Allen would let her know Jen had called. They chatted for a few minutes. Then they hung up.

Jen thought of another friend: Tory. They had only been casual friends. She tapped her fingers against her phone. *Why not?* Quickly, she texted Tory's number. No reply came. Jen decided to call her. To her surprise, Tory answered.

"This is Victoria."

"Tory?" Jen said. "Hey, it's Jen. Jen Conrad."

A long, uncomfortable pause followed.

"Oh," Tory finally said. "Hello, Jen."

The next few minutes were awkward. Tory went by Victoria now. She had moved to Rhode Island. Her first semester at Brown University was underway. High school felt like a lifetime ago to her. She claimed to have lost touch with their mutual friends.

"So," Tory said with a snicker. "How are you coping with the bad press?"

The words were spoken like a true "frenemy." Jen did not respond.

Tory continued. "It must be awful. Some say you killed that model in Japan. Then you hid her body." Jen was silent while Tory talked. "But don't worry. I don't think that. My money is on you."

"Your money?" Jen gritted her teeth. "Did you place a bet?"

Tory laughed. "Just a small one."

Jen hung up. She tossed the phone onto the bed. *Forget Tory. Was she always like that? Why did I ever hang out with her?* Kim had been a true friend. But calling Tory had been a big mistake.

She let her mind wander. *What about relationships? I've never been interested in anyone. Maybe my parents messed me up.*

Jack and Val never should have gotten married. They had eventually figured that out. Now Jack was married to Todd. Val was with Rob.

He is so creepy. What is with that guy?

Val was secretive about Rob. He had started out as her bodyguard. Then he'd become her boyfriend. Jen had googled him to learn more. But she'd found nothing.

Jen's thoughts were giving her a headache. She turned on a movie. But Jen quickly lost interest. Her mind was full. Everything was too much.

Chapter 8

LISTEN
CLOSELY

The bedroom was dark. Jen turned over. She blinked a few times. The sky outside was a deep purple. The sun had set again.

Her body ached. Moving slowly, she got out of bed. Brushing her hair took effort. It was the most she could do. *Why even bother with anything else?*

Music came from Babe's bedroom. She often kept the radio on.

Jen left her alone and walked downstairs. The beach called to her. It was her favorite place. At night, it was best.

She sat on the sand. Waves lapped at the shore. The sky soon lost its purple glow. Stars grew brighter.

Jen needed to clear her head. She breathed deep. It didn't work. Ideas about Cammie filled her mind. *What happened?* Thoughts rushed in.

Suddenly, Jen was back in a Tokyo police station.

"I don't know who he was." Jen swallowed a lump in her throat. "Just some guy. She met him the night before. I never saw him or his friends." *Why won't the police listen to me?* Jen thought.

The detective was stern. "How many men were there?"

"I don't know."

"Where did Cammie meet them?"

Jen shrugged. "Probably a bar or a club."

"Well, which is it? A bar or club?"

"I don't know!" She tried not to shout. But she was frustrated. "Cammie likes to go dancing. I told you that already."

"Does she take drugs?"

Jen shook her head. "I don't think so. I've never seen her with drugs."

"She didn't share her drugs with you?"

"No! I don't think she does drugs at all." Jen shoved hair out of her face. "I've never done *any* drugs. Please. I've told you everything I know."

The questions kept coming. Jen tried to be helpful. But the cops didn't want to listen.

Finally, her chaperone arrived. It was the first time Jen and Nev had met. The woman wore a designer suit and a stern expression. Everyone in the room looked at Nev as if she were in charge.

"Do not worry about this," Nev said coolly. "Just go back to work. We have some jobs for you. The police will handle this. They'll find her."

But they never did. Instead, the police began to watch Jen. They parked in front of her apartment. She was followed everywhere. Soon, the story was leaked to the press.

Then a video went viral. It showed Jen at a photo shoot. She wore a designer gown. The dress had an odd pattern. It looked bloodstained. But it wasn't. The photographer had asked for tears. Jen had cried on cue. The video was dramatic. Gossip sites picked it up.

Jen didn't give interviews. The modeling agency tried to manage the story. Still, they were frustrated. The agency did not want bad publicity. The press printed lies. Jen felt trapped. Stress grew. Her appetite vanished. Illness followed. Jen couldn't work. Days later, the agency put her on a plane home.

The cool air shook Jen from her memories. She stood up. Her sweater felt thin against the breeze.

She turned to her right. A scream stuck in her throat.

Jen saw a man standing next to her. She was startled.

Quickly, she stepped back. *It's him!*

"Hi," the young man said. "I'm Dan."

Chapter 9

NORTH STAR

Dan was the guy from before. Jen had seen him on the beach. She laughed nervously. He had scared her.

"Hi," Jen replied.

Dan wore the same white hoodie and cutoffs. The fringe on his shorts blew in the ocean breeze. Stars in the sky shone brightly. Their light helped Jen see Dan.

Up close, Dan looked young. He did not seem much older than Jen. His skin was tan. A wide smile showcased white teeth. Thick, shaggy blond hair blew around his face. Dan was handsome. Jen sized him up. He was a California surfer dude for sure.

She did not know what to do. Finally, she sat back down.

Dan smiled. He sat next to her. But he wasn't too close. "Looks like you've got a lot on your mind," he said.

Jen raised an eyebrow. "Are you a reporter?"

A confused look crossed his face. "A reporter? Like with a newspaper?"

She laughed. *Okay. This guy is not a reporter.*

Dan's easy smile felt familiar to Jen. He seemed like an old friend. Yet Jen was sure she didn't know him.

Something about Dan made her trust him. He seemed willing to listen. First, she talked about modeling. Then the rest of her story spilled out. Stress had filled the past year. She told him all about Tokyo and Cammie.

Dan listened quietly. It was as if he had nowhere else to be. Jen felt comfortable with him.

Finally, she stopped. She felt a little embarrassed.

"I'm sorry." Jen brushed hair off her face. "I'm just going on about myself. Tell me about you."

Dan smiled and looked up at the sky. "Why are some stars brighter than others?" he asked.

She gazed up. "I don't know."

"You're one of the bright ones." He glanced at her. "I can tell."

Jen blushed. "Bright? I doubt it. My life feels pretty dim."

"I think you're like the North Star." He pointed up at it. "You shine brightly. Most stars fade. They flicker. Then they slowly burn out."

Jen was shocked. "Wow. That is so crazy. My grandmother said the same thing. Have you two been talking lately?"

Dan just chuckled.

A deep breath filled Jen's lungs. For the first time in months, she felt relaxed. The two sat without speaking. They listened to the waves cut the shoreline.

Who was this guy? If he were anyone else, Jen would think he was hitting on her. But somehow she knew he wasn't. Dan was so different. Jen felt comfortable with him. She felt as if she'd known him her whole life.

Jen looked into Dan's eyes. There was a light in them. Then she realized it was a reflection. She turned. The patio light was flashing on and off.

"I have to go. That blinking light means my grandma needs me." Jen stood up and brushed the sand off her legs. She did not want to go. "Maybe I'll see you here again."

Dan nodded. "I hope so."

He was a good listener. Jen wanted to thank him. It meant so much to her. Should she shake his hand? No. That seemed weird. What about a peck on the cheek? No, that was too forward. Finally, she turned and walked to the house. It took everything in her not to look back.

Chapter 10

UNWANTED
VISITORS

Jen walked into the house. She called for Babe.

"Up here," her grandmother said. She sounded nervous.

Curious, Jen climbed the staircase. Babe led her to one of the guest rooms. It faced the front of the house. She opened the curtain a crack. Jen peered out the window. Two men stepped out of a black car. They walked toward the house.

"Who are they?" Jen asked. "Isn't that Rob's car over there? Is he here too?"

Babe and Jen watched the men go to a door. It led to the lower level.

"I think Rob is in the downstairs gym," Babe said. "I hate this. Val and Rob let strangers into my home. At all hours! I'll have to speak to your mother about this."

"I'll talk to Rob," Jen said.

A car door slammed. They looked out the window again. The two men had returned to the car. It sped off down the driveway.

"I'll be right back." Jen marched to the lower level. She walked down the dark hallway to the gym. The door was locked.

"Boo!" a voice behind her called out.

Jen spun around. She pressed her back against the door. It was Rob. He stood over her. His grin showed stained yellow teeth. The tight black T-shirt he wore was not flattering. His muscles were big. But so was his belly. Maybe he'd been attractive once. There was little sign of that now.

Rob was a jerk. Jen did not understand what Val saw in him.

"What do you want?" Rob asked, leaning close to her.

"Why is this door locked?"

"It's always locked. This is my space."

"Since when?" Jen tried to keep her voice steady.

"This is my office."

"*Your* office?" she asked. "It's Babe's old gym."

Rob crossed his arms. "Yes. My office. Val and I made a deal with your grandma. I'm a personal trainer. I have clients. Stay out of here."

Jen pushed past him. He grabbed her thin arm. "You know, Jen. You're too nosy. If you know what's good for you, you will leave me alone. I don't bother you. Don't bother me." His smirk made her skin crawl. "You already have enough trouble. Right?"

Disgusted, she jerked her arm from his grasp. "Don't ever touch me again," Jen hissed. Quickly, she turned and walked away.

"Enjoy your time here, sweetheart," he called out. "Because you won't be here much longer."

Jen ran upstairs. A shower sounded good. She needed to scrub her arm where Rob had touched her. First, she would talk to Babe. She would let her know Rob was downstairs.

His comment rang in her head. *"You won't be here much longer."*

What was he planning?

Chapter 11

FRESH AIR

The next day came. To her surprise, Jen woke easily. Today was her last day of being 17. She did not want to celebrate her birthday tomorrow. But turning 18 should mean something. At least that was what she'd thought years ago.

She wanted to confront her mom about Rob. Babe didn't like people coming in and out of her home. Anger washed over Jen. She had to protect Babe. Her grandmother should feel safe in her own home.

Jen dressed. She took the time to choose a decent outfit and put on makeup. It had been weeks since she'd done this. The press might still be after her. *If I'm selling magazines, I might as well look good.*

After she was ready, Jen knocked on Babe's bedroom door. There was no answer. Jen opened it slowly. Babe was painting near the wall of windows.

"Sorry to bother you," Jen said softly.

Babe turned to her. "Come in."

"May I borrow your car?" Jen asked. "Mom is at the TV studio today. I need to talk to her."

"Of course," Babe said. "Be careful. That old Benz hasn't been driven in a while. I'm not sure what shape it's in. But it should be able to get you to LA."

"It will be fine."

"Do you think it's too soon?" Babe asked. "I mean, the press and all. Is it safe for you to go out?"

Jen hesitated. "I think so. There aren't photographers near the house anymore. Maybe I'm old news. It is Hollywood after all."

Babe smiled and set down her paintbrush. Then she walked over to the dresser. She picked up the car keys. "Drive safely. Call if you need anything."

Jen hugged her grandmother. "Thanks."

NO SELFIES PLEASE

Jen's drive to the city was uneventful. She kept checking to make sure no one was following her. The coast was clear.

The tower of Starlight Television Studios appeared ahead. Jen pulled up to the gate. The lot held fond memories. Her dad had worked there many times. Once, she'd watched him fall from a tall building. It was for a cop show. She had only been six or seven.

"Miss?" the security guard called out. "Miss!"

Jen slowly drove the car to the gatehouse. She rolled down the window. "I'm here to see Val Kane."

The man stared at his clipboard. "Which show?" he asked.

"*Love and Law*. It's taping on Lot Seven."

"Do you have an appointment?" he asked.

"No," she said. "But she'll see me. I'm her daughter."

He still had not looked at her. "Name?"

She tried to smile. "Jen. Jen Conrad."

The guard picked up his phone. Then he hesitated. Finally, he looked up. His eyes squinted at her. "Wait a minute." He studied her. "*You're* Jen Conrad?"

Jen dropped her phony smile. She nodded warily. "Yes. Please open the gate."

Now the guard smiled. "Hey, I know you. I read about you. You're that model. They think you killed your friend over in China. Or Japan? Can I get a selfie? It isn't against the rules. You don't work here."

Jen put the car in reverse. She drove back onto the street. Then she turned and sped away. The drive home was a blur. Her mind raced. When would this story die?

Is this my life now? Ugh.

She drove back to Malibu. The beach house was safe as long as Rob was not around. Once there, she curled up in bed.

♕

When Jen woke from her nap, the bedroom glowed a deep orange. The sun was setting. The beach looked inviting. She threw on comfortable clothes then stopped. *What if Dan is out there? I can't look like this.*

Jen tied her hair into a neat ponytail. Then she brushed her teeth and fixed her makeup. The beach was empty. Dan was not there. The sun had almost completely disappeared. Jen felt the breeze against her face. Sinking into the sand, she tried to relax. But her thoughts raced.

What was up with that guard? He should be fired.

Rob was worse, though. He was so gross. She needed to figure out his story.

Jen's thoughts drifted to Dan. Who was he? She pulled the necklace out from under her sweater. The metal felt warm between her fingers. The gold heart seemed too sentimental. Jen suddenly felt embarrassed. *What am I doing out here? Why am I waiting for this guy? This is silly.*

She stood and brushed sand from her jeans. Jen needed to forget about Dan. Rob was the problem. Her mom was not safe with him. No one was.

He was up to something. Jen was going to find out what.

Chapter 13

JUNK DRAWER

The alarm rang. But Jen was already awake. It was a morning of firsts since returning from Japan. This was the first time she'd set her alarm. It was also the first time she'd felt purposeful.

She checked her phone. No messages appeared. Her parents had not called with birthday wishes. *I guess this is what it feels like to be 18. Happy birthday to me.*

Her grandmother slept in most mornings. Later, Babe would wish her a happy birthday.

Jen took a quick shower and dressed. Babe's car keys were still in her bag. That was good. She needed to get to the city.

The Pacific Coast Highway was jammed with cars. That was nothing new. Everyone wanted to get to LA. It was the best route. The freeway would be a parking lot.

Jen yawned. A mocha might help wake her up. Her favorite coffee shop was close by. She decided to exit the highway. The shop's drive-through was a safe bet. Jen ordered her drink. She smiled after picking up her mocha. No one had recognized her.

Maybe it would be a good day after all. It felt almost normal. Jen was like a regular commuter. She sipped her coffee as she drove.

Once in LA, Jen headed to Val's condo. Her mom would be on set. Rob should be at work with her. But there were no guarantees.

Jen was on a mission. She was in search of answers. What kind? She was not sure.

The lobby of her mother's building looked updated. The walls had been painted. There was new furniture. Jen had lived there once. But it felt like a lifetime ago. Only the doorman was the same.

"Hey, Steve." Jen smiled as she walked past him.

"Hello, Miss Conrad," he said. "I haven't seen you in some time. Where have you been hiding?"

"Oh, just traveling. It's good to see you. Take care."

Jen walked quickly to the elevators. There was a slot near the buttons. She slid in her old key card. It still worked. *Yes!* This meant the front door would open too.

When she got to her mom's floor, Jen checked the hallway. No one was around. Quickly, she unlocked the door. Then she slipped into the condo. A gasp caught in her throat. Clothes were tossed over furniture. Ashtrays were filled. Trash littered the dining room table. Dirty dishes were piled in the kitchen sink.

The place was a mess. That was odd. Val had a cleaning service. She hated housework. But she was a clean freak.

Jen walked into her old bedroom. Her bed was gone. In its place was a desk and chair. An old loveseat was in the corner. Val had moved Rob in. Jen was clearly out.

In the closet, most of her clothes were gone. A few of her things were crammed in the back. Jen was furious.

She sat at the desk. Papers covered the surface. This was her chance to find out something about Rob. She opened the top drawer. There was a large envelope. Inside was a legal document. It was Val's will. Jen began to read. Val had left her entire estate to Rob.

Jen's jaw dropped. The will was new. It was dated the week before she'd returned from Tokyo. The signature line was blank. Her mother had not signed it.

Jen opened other drawers. There was a lot of junk. But in the bottom drawer was a black leather box. She lifted the lid. The contents made her feel sick.

NO ESCAPE

The box contained jewelry. It was all Val's. But there was a problem. Some of the pieces were barely recognizable. The stones were missing. Jen picked up a ring. The setting was familiar. It was the engagement ring Jack had given her mother. Except there was a gaping hole where the diamond should be. Jen picked up a necklace. It used to be filled with dark blue sapphires. Now it had shiny pink stones. They looked cheap.

A velvet bag in the box caught her attention. Jen set the necklace down. She dumped out the contents of the bag. Jewels of all sizes poured out. When she looked closer, she understood. These weren't jewels. They were cheap glass. Jen was no expert. But even she could tell they weren't real. There had to be at least 20 different stones. One looked like a fake diamond to fit Val's ring.

Jen couldn't believe it. But it all made sense.

Suddenly the front door opened. Jen quickly put the box back and closed the drawer. Where could she hide? Her eyes darted around her old room. There was no escape.

She heard a voice in the living room. It was a man. But it did not sound like Rob. The person was coming closer. Jen squeezed behind the bedroom door.

"Where is it?" the man asked. He was on the phone. "I looked on the bookshelf. There isn't a large envelope. It's not on the dining room table either."

He stepped into the office. Jen froze. She held her breath.

The man moved papers on the desk. "It's not here," he said.

Jen started to sweat. *Please don't see me.* She did not dare breathe. The man must be looking for the will. *Who is he talking to?*

"Listen, dude," the man said, raising his voice. "Don't believe me? Come here and look for it."

He must be speaking to Rob, Jen thought. *This guy has to be one of his thugs.*

The man left the office. A few minutes later, the front door slammed. He was gone.

Jen let out her breath. She slowly walked into the living room. Her phone was in her purse. She called her mother. Val did not answer.

Jen texted her. "Need to talk. Urgent! Where are you?"

Again, there was no response. Next, Jen called the studio.

A woman answered. "Starlight TV. How may I direct your call?"

"Val Kane, please. The *Love and Law* set on Lot Seven. This is her daughter, Jen. It's an emergency."

"One moment."

The phone rang again. Seconds later, the call connected. A staff member answered.

"Sorry, Jen," she said. "Val didn't work today."

Jen sighed and thanked her. She was about to hang up.

"Oh, wait." the woman added. "One more thing. Would you do us a favor? Val parked in a tow zone. I don't know why she didn't park in her reserved spot. When you find her, would you ask her to move her car?"

Something was wrong. Jen could feel it. This was the same sense of dread she'd felt in Japan.

Maybe Val was at the beach house. Jen called Babe. Her grandmother did not have a cell phone. She did not believe in answering machines either. Babe did like her caller ID, though. But there was no answer. Babe's phone kept ringing.

Jen panicked. She headed back to the beach house. Fear started to take over. What would she find?

The drive to Malibu took forever. Jen pulled the car into the driveway. Rob's car was there. Jen's heart dropped. Fear overwhelmed her.

She jumped out of the car and bolted into the house. "Babe? Babe!" Jen called out. The house was silent.

She sprinted upstairs. Babe's bedroom was at the end of the hall. A sliver of light shone from underneath the closed door. Jen walked slowly toward the room. A groan came from inside.

She pushed open the door. The curtains were drawn. It was dark. Her hand reached for the light switch. The room lit up. Val was on the bed.

"Mom?" Jen rushed toward her. "What are you doing here?"

Val was still.

Jen leaned over. Her mother opened her eyes and gave Jen a dazed smile.

FAME MONSTER

Mom!" Jen screamed when Val closed her eyes again. She gently shook her mother. Val's body was limp. "Mom, wake up. Wake up!"

Val groaned again. Her eyes opened. She grinned and tried to focus. Jen pushed her mother's hair off her face.

"There's my sweet baby girl. Val lifted her head. I'm so . . . sorry." Her body went limp again.

"Mom! Can you hear me?" Jen shook her mother. "Where is Rob?"

Val began to cry. "I'm sorry, baby," she sobbed. "I'm so sorry. I'm a bad mother. I failed you. Fame is fake. I'm a fake. A nobody. I'm worthless."

A nightstand was next to the bed. On it was a water bottle. It was half full. But it didn't look like water. Jen studied it. Cloudy liquid filled the bottle. White, powdery residue covered the bottom.

Oh no! "Did Rob drug you? Mom! Answer me. Did he do this to you?"

"Rob's right," Val mumbled. "I'm a terrible person."

Jen fumed. "Where is he? Where is that jerk?"

"Here I am."

Jen whipped around. Rob was standing in the doorway. His left arm was around Babe's shoulders. A gun was in his right hand.

Val passed out.

Babe's eyes widened. "I think he put something in her water," she said. "I tried to call 911."

Rob spoke calmly. "Don't worry, sweetheart. Val will be fine. She'll come around. But you two will not be here to see it."

Jen stood very still. She looked Rob in the eyes. "I found her will. And I found the jewelry. I know what you're trying to do." She glanced at Babe. "He's been taking the gems out of Mom's jewelry." Her eyes darted back to Rob. "You're selling them and keeping all the money. Aren't you? And what about the will?" Jen was disgusted. "Is hocking jewelry too small time for you? Now you're just trying to steal Mom's whole estate?"

Rob pointed the gun at Jen. "You are more trouble than you're worth. You know that? The world thinks you're a washed-up model. A killer. Now I'm going to prove it. This is how it's going down. Val will wake up. She'll find you dead. Babe will be dead from—"

Suddenly, Babe swung her left arm up. She jabbed her fingers into Rob's eyes. Quickly, the older woman pushed away from him.

"Babe," Jen yelled. "No!"

Rob cried out in pain. Then he grabbed Babe. She started to jab at him again. Rob pushed her away. She fell back against a bureau. Babe crumpled to the ground.

Jen started to run toward her grandmother. But Rob lunged for Jen. She went down hard. The impact knocked the air out of her.

Rob stumbled a bit. He pulled a chair to him. Then he picked Jen up like a ragdoll. He put her in the chair.

Long cords hung on the window blinds. He grabbed them and yanked. Jen was too stunned to struggle. Rob tied her to the chair. Then he swore and left the room.

Chapter 16

MOONLIGHT
SWIM

Jen slowly shook her head. It throbbed. Her hands tingled.

Babe was still on the floor. Val was on the bed. She was unconscious.

This was not going well. Rob was going to kill them all. Jen had to do something.

I've got to get out of here. She tried to think. Her purse was in the car. The envelope was there too. That was her only proof.

Her fingers fumbled with the ties. Rob could return at any second. Jen shook her arms. Then she wiggled her hands. The cords loosened. Soon she was free.

First, she ran to her grandmother.

Babe's eyes were opening. "I'm okay," she said. "Get help. Call 911."

Rob was somewhere in the house. Jen knew it. But she did not know where. Quickly, she looked around. Val's phone had to be there. Her mother's purse was on the bed. Jen moved fast. She turned the purse upside down. The contents fell out. But there was no phone. Time was against her. She had to get help.

Jen peered down the hallway. There was no sign of Rob. She ran to the stairs. Pausing, she looked down. The living room was empty.

Jen tried to pump herself up. *Get out the front door. You can do this.*

Her head pounded. She heard footsteps. Rob was coming. He was on the lower level. Jen glanced at the living room below. She didn't see him. But the front door was too far. He would easily catch her. The patio door was closer.

Jen raced down the stairs. Then she pulled on the patio door. It did not budge.

Bang!

Rob had fired his gun. The bullet just missed her. He was across the living room.

Jen tugged on the door again. Finally, it opened. She ran across the patio.

The moon was full. The sand glowed in the moonlight. Jen was an easy target. Panicked, she searched for a place to escape.

The house behind her lit up. Rob was turning on all the lights. There was no escaping down the beach. He would see her.

Only one option was left. Jen took off. A shot rang out. Her feet stumbled. Then she gained traction. Jen ran toward the breaking waves.

Holding her breath, she dove into a wave. Her head throbbed. What would happen when she surfaced? Would Rob see her?

Jen came up for air. Immediately, she went under again. Now she was beyond the surf line. The water was calmer. She surfaced again, gasping for air. Rob was on the shore, looking at the waves. He did not notice the person coming up behind him.

It was Babe.

FOREVER YOUNG

Don't move!" Babe shouted. The waves could not swallow her voice. She pointed a gun at Rob.

He stood still for a second. Then he turned and started to raise his gun.

Bang! Bang!

At first, Jen could not tell who fired the shots. Then Babe fell to the sand. The gun dropped from her hand. Before Jen could react, Rob slumped to his knees. Then he fell face first in the sand. Babe's bullet had hit him.

Jen was stunned. Her grandmother had fierce inner strength. She'd found her gun and made her way outside.

Fighting the surf, Jen crawled from the water. "Babe!" she screamed.

Jen ran to her grandmother. Gently, she pulled Babe onto her lap. There was some blood on her head. But it was not a bullet wound. She had not been shot.

Babe looked up at her granddaughter. She smiled softly. "My heart is old. I'm afraid it's not up for this."

"Hang in there," Jen said. "Please stay with me. I will get help. Okay?" The necklace she'd found dangled from her neck.

Babe reached out and touched it. "Where?" she whispered. "Where did you get this?" The gold heart caught the moonlight. "I thought I had lost it forever."

"What?" Jen glanced down at the necklace. "This is yours? I found it on the beach."

Babe turned the heart over. There was an inscription: FOR E.K. Jen had never noticed it before.

"E.K.," Jen said. "Of course! Emma Kane."

"He gave it to me," her grandmother said.

"Who?"

Babe turned her head. As she looked toward the water, her eyes widened. She pointed a shaky finger. "Dan. Dear God! Dan, is that you?"

Jen turned, and there he was. Dan stood near the shore. He was wearing the same white hoodie and cutoffs. His blond hair moved with the breeze. He smiled at the two women.

Babe smiled back. A look of joy spread across her face. "My love."

Jen was stunned. *What is happening?*

Babe suddenly closed her eyes. She went limp.

"No," Jen cried. "No! Wait. Please don't go."

A scream caught in her throat. "Dan!" she called out. "Help me."

But Dan had vanished.

Chapter 18

OLD FRIENDS

The press had a field day. They loved the Hollywood gossip. Tabloids covered the story. The headlines were not surprising.

"Val Kane: Mental Illness and Murder"

"A Hollywood Family Tragedy"

"Jen Conrad: Serial Murderer?"

"Model Daughter or Deadly Daughter?"

Jen had taken it in stride. No interviews were given. Only the family's lawyers made statements.

Then the gossip really took off. The truth about Cammie came out. Police found her alive. She had run off with a guy in Tokyo. Later, they married in Greece. Cammie had been tired of modeling. She'd vanished so she could start fresh.

Jen was cleared.

Her anger surfaced. But it quickly disappeared. She was not mad at Cammie. Jen understood wanting a new start. Plus, she needed to focus on her family.

Saying goodbye to Babe was hard. There hadn't been a funeral. Babe had not wanted one. Instead, a golden urn held her ashes. The urn sat below the Hockney painting. She would have loved that. Jen was sure of it.

Staring at the painting, Jen wiped away a tear. Babe had given her so much love. Jen wanted to make her proud.

The doorbell rang. It pulled Jen from her thoughts. *Who could that be?* she wondered. *Reporters know not to come to the door.*

Jen steeled herself. *Expect the unexpected.*

She threw open the door. Her jaw dropped. "Kim?"

KEEPING PROMISES

A smile lit up Kim's face. She had not changed since high school. "Hey. I'm sorry to just show up. I got back in town today. Mom told me about Babe. Are you okay? You two were so close. I wanted to make sure—"

Jen did not let her finish. She wrapped her arms around Kim in a bear hug. "I'm so happy to see you. I tried to call." She led Kim inside. They sat on the couch.

Kim pushed back her dark hair. "I took a gap year. My aunt invited me to stay with her in France. I got a new phone there." She squeezed Jen's hands. "I'm so sorry. I wasn't here when you needed me. Tell me everything."

Jen needed someone to talk to. But she had not realized how much. The flood gates opened. She started talking and couldn't stop. Everything poured out. Words tumbled over each other. Finally, she stopped and took a breath.

"I'm so glad your mom's okay," Kim exclaimed. "I know she was horrible to you. But it wasn't all her fault."

Jen agreed. "No. It wasn't. She has never been the best mother. But Rob made it worse. It would have been different lately if not for him."

A hopeful smile crossed Kim's face. "Maybe there's still time for her to change."

Jen nodded. "I hope so. She's out of the hospital. But she's going to spend time at a new place. It's like mental health rehab. She finally wants to take control of her bipolar disorder. It's kind of weird to see her being responsible."

"That's wonderful!" Kim's eyes sparkled. "There is another reason I'm here. I thought you might need a place to stay. I'm getting my own apartment. Let's be roomies!"

Jen grinned. "I would love to. But I have a place to stay." She waved her arm around. "This place! The beach house!"

Kim gaped at her. "You're staying here?"

"I sure am!" Jen said.

The beach house was hers. Babe had left it to Jen. It

suited her. The quiet was comforting. Her grandmother had lived there for years. Jen knew why. The place felt like a warm hug.

"Babe's spirit is alive here," Jen said. "She may be gone. But I feel close to her in this house. It's a good feeling."

Kim patted Jen's hand. "She will always be with you. No matter where you are. But you can't be a hermit. I won't let that happen. We'll spend more time together. You need to live. Put yourself out there. Stop being afraid."

Thoughts of the future excited Jen. "You're right. I need to live my life. And I want it full of happiness. You might have to help me with that."

Kim's hand went over her heart. "I promise."

Chapter 20

GONE BUT NOT FORGOTTEN

Months passed. Jen focused on her blessings. She made up with her dad. They were working on trust. It would take her a while. But Jack was trying. That was a start. At least they were speaking again. He had even visited Val.

Jen's mother had gone through a lot. She'd spent six months in the mental health facility. Jen spoke to her every day. The star had been fired from *Love and Law*. She feared her acting days were over. Lucky for Val, Hollywood had a short memory. Now she was out of rehab. Work offers were pouring in. There was no such thing as bad publicity.

Kim had become a true friend. She was smart and kind. Jen spent a lot of time with her. The girl was not a

Hollywood type at all.

Jen focused on school. She even earned her GED. Maybe college was next. First, she wanted to decide on a career. Astronomy interested her. She'd even bought a telescope.

One day, Kim surprised her with a book. It was about the galaxy. Kim had even written a quote in the book.

"Norman Vincent Peale said it best. 'Shoot for the moon. Even if you miss, you'll land among the stars.'"

Jen smiled at the quote. Her life was changing. It was getting better.

Modeling wasn't her passion. She would never return to it. Jen wanted to find her place in the world. She had many new interests to explore. Money was not a problem. Babe had left her a large trust fund. Jen had saved too.

One day, Jen went into the garage. It had been Babe's art studio years ago. Paintings filled much of the space. Jen dug through them. A familiar face surprised her. It was a watercolor of Dan.

Jen would never know for sure what had happened on the beach with him. But she was glad Dan had been in Babe's life.

Several more paintings of Dan were in the garage. Babe had painted him many times. What would have happened if he had lived? At least he and Babe were together now. Jen was sure of it.

She left the garage as it was. Later, she would return. Cleaning it up could wait. Now it was time for her evening ritual.

The sun glowed bright red as it set over the Pacific. Jen watched it disappear. What a year it had been. Cammie's disappearance had been terrible. But at least she was safe.

The incident with Rob had hurt Jen deeply. Yet it had brought her and Val together.

Losing Babe had been the worst of all.

Still, Jen had come out on the other side. Now she was ready to let her star shine.

WANT TO KEEP
READING?

9781680215977

Turn the page for a sneak peek
at another book in the Monarch
Jungle series.

Chapter 1

THE BASEMENT

Usually, I pay no attention when objects go missing. They're probably just in a moving box. Small items disappear first. Maybe it's a book, DVD, or my track hoodie. Then bigger things vanish. Mom's datebook is gone without a trace. Dad's tools also pull a disappearing act. Almost every day, something goes missing. It's annoying. Now the air conditioner is broken. That's even worse.

I think our new house is haunted. Maybe the ghost wants to be noticed. The house is more than 100 years old. Most of the houses in this New Jersey town are ancient. That's why my parents like it. It's why I don't.

Mom has been on my back. She wants me to do laundry. I hate laundry. The washer and dryer are in the basement. That place is creepy. It's so dark and damp. Spiderwebs are everywhere. I don't like going down there. It feels like I'm walking into a horror movie.

My mom has no sympathy for me. Today is Saturday. A basket of dirty laundry waits for me. It sits by the basement door. I flip on the light switch. A dim bulb flickers.

The narrow stairway creaks as I make my way down. A moldy smell makes me gag. My feet move slowly on the steps. All I think of is the last scary movie I saw.

From under the stairs, a hand could reach out. It could grab me. With each step, I wait for it.

The ceiling is too low. I almost bump my head. It feels like spiders are crawling through my hair. The floor is concrete. Bricks make up the walls.

A room in the back corner freaks me out. The door is always closed. I went in there once. This room has a dirt floor. The walls are wooden. It doesn't match the rest of the concrete basement. Lying on the floor is a shovel. Maybe it was used to bury a body. Sometimes I think about digging around to find out.

This spooky house looks like one in a horror movie. The basement just confirms it.

I can't keep my eyes off the door to the back room. Sometimes I swear the knob turns on its own. Sounds come from inside. That can't be possible though. It must be in my head. Still, it's enough to scare me.

I dump the basket of clothes into the washer. Then I pour in more than enough soap. Mom tells me I should separate the colors. But why?

Well, one time I turned Mom's white blouse pink. But that was the fault of my red shorts. Dad's new white socks turned gray once. That was only because I washed them with new jeans. Nothing red or new is in this load. It should all be good. One load is better than three. I'm saving time and money.

I close the washing machine lid. Then I look around. I'm alone. Boxes are stacked everywhere. Nothing stirs. Noises come from above me. Mom is moving around upstairs. Yet my brain tells me something is down here with me. I turn the knob on the washer. Next, I press start.

Slowly, I walk to the stairs. Then I stop. Is something coming out of the dark at me? My eyes dart around. The light flickers again. Now I run for the stairs. I leave whatever is down there in my dust. At the top of the stairs, I throw the door open. It slams shut behind me.